# THE                    IME

Spencer drew me close, taking both my hands in his.

"Thank you for dinner," I told him, gazing up into his bright blue eyes. "Everything was just perfect."

"No, not quite," he said. "There's still one thing missing."

"What?"

For an answer, Spencer bent his head and kissed me gently on the lips. "That," he murmured.

Hearing no argument from me, he kissed me again, more thoroughly this time. For a moment, it was just like a dream. Then reality reared its ugly head as Spencer whispered into my ear, "You're really a special girl, Clarissa."

He might as well have thrown a bucket of cold water in my face. It was terrible to hear myself called by someone else's name at such a romantic moment.

**Bantam titles in the Sweet Dreams series. Ask your bookseller for titles you have missed:**

# THE CINDERELLA GAME

## Sheri Cobb South

BANTAM BOOKS

NEW YORK · TORONTO · LONDON · SYDNEY · AUCKLAND

# THE CINDERELLA GAME
## A BANTAM BOOK 0 553 29454 7

First publication in Great Britain

PRINTING HISTORY
Bantam edition published 1993

Bantam Books are published by Transworld Publishers Ltd., 61–63 Uxbridge Road, Ealing, London W5 5SA, in Australia by Transworld Publishers (Australia) Pty. Ltd., 15–25 Helles Avenue, Moorebank, NSW 2170, and in New Zealand by Transworld Publishers (N.Z.) Ltd., 3 William Pickering Drive, Albany, Auckland.

Printed and bound in Great Britain by
Cox & Wyman Ltd., Reading, Berks.

# THE
# CINDERELLA
# GAME

# One

"I guess I ate too much at last night's charity banquet," Jillian Reed, Virginia's Teen Beauty, confessed. "When the mayor told a joke, I split my seams laughing—literally! Do you think you can fix it?"

"I think so," I said, inspecting the frayed seam of her red taffeta dinner dress. "I'll do my best, anyway."

Jillian let out a sigh of relief. "Wendy, you're a lifesaver!"

"If you win, just remember me in your victory speech when you thank all the 'little people,' " I told her.

"I'll do that," she promised with a laugh. "Thanks!"

A moment later she was gone, leaving me alone in the tiny backstage sewing room I shared with Mrs. Crowley and Mrs. Evans, the two other pageant seamstresses. I couldn't help smiling as I surveyed the cluttered room, with its sewing machines, dress forms, and piles of clothing covering every available surface. My hometown of Bellevue isn't exactly the summer employment capital of the world, so I couldn't believe it when my best friend, Kim, got us both summer jobs with the nationally acclaimed America's Teen Beauty Pageant, Bellevue's only claim to fame.

Of course, it helped to have friends in high places. Kim's aunt worked as a receptionist at pageant headquarters. At first Kim had felt a little guilty about landing a position as an office assistant while I worked backstage at the Coliseum as a seamstress, but I didn't mind. In fact, I wouldn't have traded places with her for anything. I loved all the bustle and excitement, as well as the close contact with the contestants and their managers, talent coaches, hairdressers, and makeup artists. Sometimes it was hard to believe that these beautiful, talented girls were only seventeen years old—exactly my own age.

As I pinned the rip in Jillian's dress, my mind drifted back to the day Mom first taught me to sew. I was only ten years old at the time, and the very thought of guiding the fabric underneath the flying needle scared me to death. But Mom had insisted that it would come in handy someday, and she was right. I was soon making almost all my own clothes, and I pride myself on my ability to dress stylishly without spending a fortune.

*But I'll bet even Mom never imagined this,* I thought with a smile as I threaded my sewing machine. At this very minute, I could be repairing the wardrobe of the future America's Teen Beauty. I admit this was tedious work sometimes, but still it was the most glamorous, exciting job I'd ever had.

"Wendy! Wendy Miller, where *are* you?"

Recognizing the voice, I heaved a sigh and pushed the dress aside. I guess every job has its drawbacks, and in this case, the drawback was Clarissa Devoe, Florida's Teen Beauty. She seemed to think I had nothing to do but wait on her personally, even though there were contestants from all fifty states, D.C., and Puerto Rico, with dresses to be ironed, rips to be mended, and hems to be raised or lowered. Mrs. Evans and Mrs. Crowley were far more experienced than I was, but that didn't seem to bother Clarissa. She had appointed me as her servant, probably because I was her own age and easier to bully.

"*There* you are! I've been looking all over for you!" Clarissa said as she came into the sewing room.

"What is it this time, Clarissa?" I asked, prepared for the worst.

"I need you to have these things cleaned for me. This is for tomorrow night's chamber of commerce banquet," she said, dumping a floral print dress onto my lap, "and this is for my interview next week, and this—"

"Hold it!" I said as she added a white linen suit to the pile on my lap. "Didn't I have this cleaned for you just yesterday?"

"Yes, but the collar and sleeves look wilted!

4

Make them do it again, and tell them to double up on the starch. And one more thing—"

She handed me a long strip of white satin ribbon bearing the word "Florida" in black letters. I recognized it at once: It was the sash she wore to identify her home state. Each contestant was given two sashes, one for day-to-day wear and the other in case the first one got lost or dirty. Looking at the sash more closely, I noticed that it was covered with light brown spots.

"Tea stains," Clarissa said with disgust. "At last night's charity banquet, some idiot waiter splashed tea all over me. See if the dry cleaner's can get it out, will you?"

"Yes, your highness. Of course I can take it to the cleaner's," I muttered aloud after she had left. "I've got nothing better to do."

I piled Clarissa's clothes on one end of the ironing board, then went back to work on Jillian's red taffeta. It didn't take long to mend, and soon I was free to meet Kim for lunch. But first, I had a delivery to make.

A week ago I had never even set foot inside Spotless Dry Cleaner's, but now it seemed like my second home. Part of my job was the task of hauling clothes from the Coliseum to the cleaner's and back again, and soon I had come to know Mrs. Williams, the proprietress, pretty well. She always spoke her mind, and I had a feeling she would be less than pleased to see Clarissa's suit for the second time in two days.

I was right.

"We cleaned and pressed this suit only yesterday!" she said indignantly. "I remember it perfectly—I did it myself!"

"I know you did, Mrs. Williams, and I think you did a beautiful job," I assured her. "The girl just wants a little more starch in the collar and sleeves, that's all. She's sort of—well, finicky."

"Finicky, hmph! *I* could give you another name for it! If a girl like that can win the national title, well, there's just no justice in this world. It seems to me that a nice and pretty girl like *you* should be out there winning beauty contests instead of running yourself ragged waiting on some of those awful girls."

"No, not me," I said quickly. "I'm not the beauty-contest type. I'm happier backstage."

Mrs. Williams sighed. "Well then, stop by in the morning about nine o'clock and I should have these things done for you."

"Great! I'll pick them up on my way to work. Thanks a lot, Mrs. Williams. You make my job a lot easier!"

That taken care of, I hopped into my car, ready for a well-deserved lunch break. But as I turned the key in the ignition, I discovered that my gas gauge was close to empty. There would be no lunch for me until I filled up my tank. I might be late meeting Kim, but at least I wouldn't have to walk back to work.

I drove slowly down the street, keeping an eye out for a service station, and I found one on the next block. I turned in and parked in front of the self-service pump, but when I tried to remove the cap from the gas tank, it wouldn't budge. I turned and twisted it with all my might, but it was no use.

"Got a problem?" said a voice behind me.

Turning around, I saw a boy of about seventeen or eighteen with light brown hair and the bluest eyes I had ever seen.

"It's stuck," I said helplessly.

I stepped aside to give him room. He

grabbed the cap and gave it a firm twist to the left. There was a long hissing sound as the cap came off in his hand.

"Thanks," I said, feeling a little foolish. "I don't know how I managed to get it on that tight in the first place."

"It's the heat," he explained. "As the temperature rises, the pressure in the tank builds, and makes the cap fit tighter. Fill 'er up?"

"Oh, you don't have to do that," I said quickly.

"Hey, it's not every day that I get to rescue a damsel in distress," he said with a grin. "Don't disappoint me."

"Well, okay," I said, then remembered that I had only ten dollars in my purse. "But just five dollars' worth," I said.

As the boy pumped the gas, I went inside to pay for it. After standing outside in the hot July sun, the air-conditioned building felt good. Apparently I wasn't the only one who thought so—the place seemed to be filled with teenage guys, most of them buying soft drinks.

"Five dollars on pump four," I said when I

reached the front of the line, then blinked as I recognized the girl at the cash register. "Maggie! What are you doing here?"

She grinned at me. "Hey, Wendy. What does it look like I'm doing? I'm working here over the summer. What about you? Did you ever find a job? Before school let out you said you were going to look for one."

"I got a temporary one, at least," I answered. "I'm helping the seamstresses backstage at the Teen Beauty pageant."

Maggie was impressed. "Wow! Lucky you!"

"I don't know about that," I said. "Your job has some terrific fringe benefits!"

"Like what?"

"Like that," I said, nodding at the door as four guys left with their sodas.

"Oh, they're regulars," Maggie said. "They come in every day about this time."

"What about the one who's pumping my gas? Is he a regular, too?"

Maggie craned her neck around to look, but a van had parked at the nearest pump, blocking her view. "I don't know—can't see him. What does he look like?"

"Tall, slim, incredible blue eyes?"

Maggie thought a moment, then shook her head.

"Then he must not be a regular. If you'd ever seen his eyes, you'd remember him," I told her. "Well, I guess I'd better get going. I'll see you when school starts, if not before."

I hurried back to my car, eager to thank my mysterious blue-eyed helper but when I got there, he was gone. I was disappointed as I drove away.

# Two

"You'll never guess who I saw today," I told Kim over lunch. "Maggie Tucker. She's working at a gas station not far from here."

Kim wrinkled her nose in distaste. "Sounds like pretty grubby work to me. But I guess Maggie needs the money, now that her mom has quit work to go back to college."

"Well, don't be too quick to shed any tears for Maggie," I said. "The poor girl is surrounded by gorgeous guys, which is more than you can say for me. Even if there *were* any guys around the Coliseum, they would never look twice at me—not with all those Teen Beauties running around."

"I know what you mean," Kim sighed. "The only males I ever see are old enough to be my father."

"Yeah, but you've got Dave," I pointed out. "You don't need a guy."

"Oh, come on, Wendy. Nobody *needs* a guy."

"Easy for you to say. You've got one."

"Yeah, and I'll admit, Dave is nice to have around," Kim said. "But I don't *need* him. I mean, if we broke up tomorrow, it wouldn't be the end of the world."

"That's not what you said last winter, when he dumped you for Heather Draper," I reminded her.

"He didn't dump me for Heather!" Kim protested. "We both agreed to date other people. It was a mutual decision."

"Yeah, right. So mutual that you cried every day for a week," I said. "Okay, forget Dave and tell me what's happening at pageant headquarters."

"I'm glad you asked," Kim said excitedly, forgetting to be insulted. "I've been hobnobbing with the rich and famous!"

"Who?" I asked, my curiosity aroused.

"Ever heard of Albert Phyffe?"

"I think so. Isn't he the one who lives in that big mansion on the edge of town?"

"Yes, it's called The Magnolias. Mom dragged me there last year during the Historic Homes Tour. It's a beautiful place. Those Phyffes are loaded!"

"So why are they hobnobbing with you?"

Kim pretended to be offended. "I think I resent that! Anyway, they have this antique piano that they're letting the pageant borrow for the talent competition. They'll be moving it to the Coliseum tomorrow. If you get a chance, you ought to go out front and sneak a peek."

"Why?"

"Pure nosiness," she said cheerfully. "Just to get a glimpse of how the other half lives. The Phyffes have a son about our age—maybe he'll be there. I can't remember his name—Stewart, or Stanley, or something like that. He graduated last spring from a posh private school."

"How do you know so much about the Phyffe family, anyway?" I asked.

"The society pages! Don't you ever read the newspaper?"

I made a face. "Yeah—especially the part that says 'Help Wanted.' "

"Well, that's taken care of, at least for the next three weeks."

Soon the wealthy Phyffe family was forgotten. Kim and I spent the rest of the lunch hour comparing notes on our new jobs.

On my way to work the next morning, I stopped by the dry cleaner's. True to her word, Mrs. Williams had all Clarissa's clothes cleaned, pressed, and covered with plastic bags to keep them immaculate. I thanked her, reminded her to send the bill to America's Teen Beauty Pageant headquarters, and headed for the door with my arms full.

"Wait a minute, honey," Mrs. Williams called just as I reached the door. Turning back, I saw her coming out from behind the counter with Clarissa's white satin sash. Since I didn't have a hand free, she looped the sash over my head in the same way the contestants wore them.

I thanked her again, hung the clothes from

the hook in the back of my car, and drove to the Coliseum. As soon as I reached the parking lot, I could tell something unusual was going on. The wide double doors were propped open, and a moving van was backed up to the entrance. A makeshift ramp of plywood and two-by-fours sloped from the back of the truck to the stage entrance. I was certainly curious—what was all the commotion for?

Then I remembered what Kim said about the Phyffes. This was the day their piano was being moved. I knew she would ask me about it later, so I parked my car, ran inside, hung Clarissa's clothes in her dressing room, then tiptoed into the wings and peeked out from behind a curtain.

There at the center of the stage was the most beautiful grand piano I had ever seen. Enormous and elaborately carved, it was obviously an antique, and a very well preserved one. I was willing to bet that it was worth more money than I would ever see in my whole lifetime. Beside it stood Mr. Carrington, the pageant director, talking to a distinguished-looking man who I assumed was Mr. Phyffe. A third man, wearing coveralls that read B & B MOVERS came onstage carrying the piano bench. He set it down, gave Mr. Carrington a receipt, and the three men left the stage together. Seizing my chance, I brushed aside the heavy velvet curtain and stepped out onto the stage. I had just reached the piano when someone behind me spoke.

"It's really something, isn't it?"

I had thought I was alone, and I nearly jumped out of my skin at the sound of a human voice. Turning quickly, I saw a boy standing less than ten feet from me—a tall, cute boy with light brown hair and unforgettable blue eyes.

"I remember you," I said. "You're the one from the gas station."

"Yeah, but I never dreamed I was pumping gas for visiting royalty," he replied.

"Who, me?" I was completely baffled, until I remembered that I was still wearing Clarissa's sash. This boy thought I was a beauty queen—Florida's Teen Beauty, to be exact! I laughed. "Oh, that! I'm not—"

"Do you play?" he asked, nodding toward the piano.

16

"A—a little. But I don't think—"

"Go ahead," he encouraged. "Play something."

I hesitated for a moment, but his smile was irresistible. I sat down on the piano bench and began to play from memory part of my last recital piece.

"Hey, not bad," he said when I had finished. "Mind if I give it a try?"

I moved over to make room for him beside me on the bench. He sat down and, after making a big show of cracking his knuckles, he played a two-finger rendition of "Chopsticks."

"Not that!" I protested. "Play something real."

"I can't," he confessed with a grin. "You've just heard my entire repertoire."

"What brings you to the Coliseum?" I asked.

"I came with the piano," he answered. "Say, what's your name? I'm Spencer—Spencer Phyffe."

I caught my breath. The boy who had pumped gas for me yesterday was none other than Spencer Phyffe, the son of one of Bellevue's wealthiest families! Kim would die if

17

she knew. Here I was, sitting at the piano with Spencer Phyffe, who thought I was Florida's Teen Beauty!

"My name is Clarissa," I replied without a moment's hesitation. "Clarissa Devoe."

# Three

I half expected to be struck by a bolt of lightning.

"Well, Clarissa, what do you think of Bellevue?" Spencer asked, unaware of my lie.

"I feel like I've lived here all my life," I said with a nervous giggle.

"Good. I hope they're not keeping you too busy to see the sights."

"Well, we have a pretty hectic schedule," I admitted. "But last Saturday they—*we*—went to visit the Scenic Gardens."

"We, or they?"

I improvised on the spot. "We were all sup- posed to go, but my flight out of Orlando was delayed, so I missed the trip." Whew! I almost sounded as if I knew what I was talking about.

"We'll have to fix that," Spencer said. "Maybe I could take you sight-seeing while you're in town."

This was either the weirdest dream I'd ever had, or the luckiest day of my life. "I—I think I'd like that," I stammered.

"Great! Why don't we start with lunch tomorrow?"

"So soon?" I asked, taken aback. I sud- denly had the feeling that things were mov- ing too fast.

"We don't have long; why waste the time we've got?" Spencer asked. "Unless you al- ready have plans for tomorrow."

I usually met Kim for lunch, but I knew she wouldn't mind if I made plans with Spen- cer. In fact, she would never forgive me if I turned him down. "Lunch tomorrow is fine," I said.

"I'll pick you up at twelve, then. Which door should I use?"

I had a horrible vision of Spencer coming backstage to find me crawling around on my knees pinning someone's hem. "Oh, you don't have to come in," I said quickly. "I can meet you out front by the fountain."

"Fine. By the way, what hotel are you staying at?"

"We don't stay in hotels. Each girl is assigned to a host family. I'm staying with Frank and Vivian Miller, in Woodland Heights." That much was true—I'd been staying with them for about seventeen years now.

"Spencer!" a man's voice called. "We're going now."

"Coming!" he answered, then turned back to me. "Don't forget, Clarissa. Tomorrow at noon, by the fountain."

"I'll be there."

After he left, my earlier doubts began to return. It felt really funny, being called by somebody else's name. I had never done anything like this in my life. I wondered what in the world had come over me. Suddenly, Clarissa's sash seemed uncomfortable around me. I slipped it over my head and dropped it onto the piano bench beside me.

*I'll set him straight tomorrow*, I thought. Spencer seemed pretty down-to-earth for somebody as rich as he was. Anybody who would pump gas for a total stranger could never be accused of snobbery. Surely it wouldn't make any difference to him that I wasn't a beauty contestant after all. In fact, we'd probably have a good laugh about the whole thing.

"Wendy!" Mr. Carrington's voice jarred me back to reality. "That piano was placed there for the contestants' use, not yours."

"Y-yes, sir," I stammered, rising quickly from the piano bench. "I only—I didn't mean—"

"I'm sure you didn't," Mr. Carrington said, more gently this time. "It's a beautiful instrument, but also a very old and valuable one. We wouldn't want to show our appreciation to the Phyffe family by damaging it, would we?"

"N-no, sir."

"Now, if you'll go backstage, I believe one of the contestants is looking for you."

I made a quick exit. *At least Mr. Carrington hadn't humiliated me in front of Spen-*

*cer,* I thought as I headed backstage, carrying Clarissa's sash. Still, the incident made me realize just how lowly my position was compared to Clarissa and the other girls. Suddenly I wasn't so sure that Spencer wouldn't mind.

As I had predicted, Kim was thrilled when I told her over lunch about my new adventure.

"You've got a date with *Spencer Phyffe?*" she said in awe.

"Shhh! You don't have to announce it to the world," I said, glancing around the Hamburger Hut.

"I don't *believe* this! What's he like?"

"He's very handsome, he's got beautiful blue eyes, and his piano playing is just plain awful."

Kim sighed. "Talk about a fairy tale come true. Spencer Phyffe, the richest guy in Bellevue, is surrounded by fifty-two beauty queens, and he chooses a seamstress!"

"Well, not exactly," I hedged.

"What do you mean?"

"I mean he doesn't exactly *know* that I'm a seamstress."

"Who does he think you are? America's Teen Beauty?" Kim teased.

"Of course not!" I cried indignantly, then added sheepishly, "he thinks I'm *Florida's* Teen Beauty."

Her eyes widened. "You're putting me on, right?"

"No. I had just come from the cleaner's with Clarissa's clothes, and I was wearing her sash, so he assumed—"

"And you let him go right on assuming," Kim said, obviously disapproving.

"Come on, Kim, lighten up! I happened to meet a guy who's nice, good looking, and filthy rich. I only wanted to make a good impression. How was I to know he would ask me out? Besides, you're the one who started it—you and your Phyffes!"

"Yeah, but I never dreamed you'd do anything this crazy!"

"To tell you the truth, I surprised myself a little," I admitted. "But it's not a crime to tell one little white lie, is it? Anyway, I'm going to set him straight, I promise."

"Oh, yeah? When?" Kim challenged.

24

"Tomorrow," I said with a lot more confidence than I felt. "Tomorrow at lunch."

The next morning was a difficult one. The contestants had been to a dinner party the night before, and the late night had made even the nicest of them cranky and irritable. Clarissa, who was cranky and irritable even on her best days, complained that the collar and sleeves of her white linen suit now felt like they'd been set in concrete. I had the feeling Mrs. Williams had gotten her revenge.

At last, twelve o'clock rolled around, and I went outside to meet Spencer. He wasn't there yet, so I sat down on the edge of the fountain, watching the traffic go by, and wondering what kind of car Spencer Phyffe might drive. As I waited, I tried to think of ways to tell him my real identity. Lost in thought, I didn't even realize Spencer had come up behind me until he spoke.

"Okay, Clarissa, ready when you are."

"Oh!" I exclaimed. "You startled me!"

"Yeah, you looked like you were off in another world."

"I guess you could say that," I replied. "To tell you the truth, I had almost given up on you."

"You think I'm going to pass up a lunch date with Florida's Teen Beauty? Not on your life!"

This did not sound promising. With a sinking heart, I remembered that at our first meeting, Spencer hadn't even hung around long enough for me to thank him properly. It wasn't until he saw me wearing Clarissa's sash that he'd shown any real interest in me.

"Sorry for the delay. It took me a while to find a parking space," Spencer explained as we threaded our way through the parking lot. "Here we are," he said as we stopped beside a bright yellow Volkswagen bug with orange flames painted on its sides.

"*This* is your car?" I said.

"My Jag is in the shop," he said, laughing, as he unlocked the passenger door and opened it for me. "Hop in."

I had wondered where a boy like Spencer would take a girl for lunch, but I never would have guessed in a million years. First we wheeled through the drive-in window at

Burgers-2-Go, then drove to a small park in the heart of the historic district. Carrying our lunch, we got out and walked through the park.

"How's this?" Spencer asked, stopping at a bench on the edge of a little lake.

I glanced around nervously, wishing he'd chosen someplace a little more private. I didn't want to take the chance of being recognized by someone I knew.

"Why don't we go over there?" I suggested, pointing to a more secluded bench under an enormous oak tree.

Spencer agreed, and we made our way to the bench and spread out our feast. The day was hot and humid, typical for Bellevue in July, but a light breeze stirred the leaves of the tree, making the heat bearable. As we ate our picnic lunch, Spencer picked sesame seeds off his hamburger bun and tossed them to the pigeons, who scrambled eagerly after them. In a nearby pavilion, a German band played a lively polka.

"Oh, look," I said to Spencer. "Isn't the music great? It makes me feel like dancing."

Spencer put down his hamburger and stood

up. "At your service," he said, bowing with exaggerated gallantry.

"Here? Now?" I asked, taken by surprise.

"Why not?"

Why not, indeed? I had always thought that romantic things like dancing in the park only happened in the movies. Nothing like that had *ever* happened to me, Wendy Miller. But they did now that I was Clarissa Devoe, Florida's Teen Beauty—at least for the moment. Smiling up at Spencer, I held out my hand and allowed him to pull me to my feet. Still holding my hand, he wrapped his other arm around my waist. Then we were off, skipping along in time to the bouncy music. By the time the song ended, we were both out of breath from laughter and exertion.

"You're pretty good," I told Spencer as we returned to our park bench. "Where did you learn to dance like that?"

"My great-aunt Edna," he replied.

"She taught you?"

"Not exactly. She thought I needed a dose of the social graces, so for my thirteenth birthday, she signed me up for lessons in

28

ballroom dancing." He grimaced. "What I really wanted was a football!"

"Poor thing," I said sympathetically. "Did you ever get to play football?"

He grinned. "No, but I *did* make the all-state polka team!"

"Well, if it's any consolation, I think you're a very good dancer."

"I'll tell Aunt Edna you said so." Spencer abruptly dropped his joking manner. "So tell me, Clarissa, do you have a regular partner?"

"No, not really," I confessed, suddenly shy. I knew that he wasn't talking about dancing.

Spencer's eyebrows rose in surprise. "No? What are all those guys in Florida thinking of, anyway?"

I wondered if I had given myself away. Somehow it was hard to imagine a girl like Clarissa sitting at home alone on a Saturday night. As I hesitated, not knowing what to say, Spencer supplied the answer I needed.

"But you must have a pretty hectic schedule as Florida's Teen Beauty. I guess it's hard to have any kind of a steady relationship, huh?"

"Exactly," I said gratefully.

I knew I had just missed the perfect opportunity to straighten out yesterday's misunderstanding. But I was having such a wonderful time—far too wonderful to spoil it all.

"So tell me about your home in Florida," Spencer said, taking another bite of his hamburger. "What's it like?"

What *was* it like, anyway? It had been years since my family had gone there on vacation. Still, Bellevue wasn't far from the Gulf Coast. Surely there couldn't be that much difference between the two places.

"Well, it's hot and humid," I said, playing it safe. "And crowded, especially in the summertime."

"Do you spend much time at the beach?"

I glanced down at my bare arms, still pale from a summer spent indoors working odd jobs. "No," I answered with perfect truth. "But I do love the water, even though I'm not much of a swimmer. In fact, I'm not much of an athlete at all. What about you?"

"Oh, I've run track for the last couple of years, but I'm hardly Olympic material. I usu-

ally like to play golf during the summer, too.
But my job has been keeping me pretty busy
this year, so I may not have time before
school starts again."

"I thought you graduated last spring," I
said without thinking.

Spencer gave me a puzzled look. "Where
did you get that idea?"

Where else? From my social-climbing best
friend, whose information was apparently
faulty. I shrugged. "I—I don't know. I just
thought you were—uh—older."

"No, just very mature for my age," he joked.

It was impossible not to smile back, but I
scolded myself mentally for being so careless.
Of course I was going to tell him the truth,
but I wanted to choose the place and time
carefully, rather than having him find out
from some silly slip of the tongue. I was more
cautious after that.

Just as I was taking the last bite of my
hamburger, I noticed Spencer looking at me,
and smiling curiously.

"You must really like ketchup," he com-
mented.

"Why?"

"Because," he said, his smile broadening into a grin, "you're wearing an awful lot of it on your chin."

"Oh!" I grabbed my paper napkin and began to scrub. "Did I get it?" I asked, presenting my chin for Spencer's inspection.

"Well, you smeared it around some. Here, let me help you."

Spencer took my chin in his hand and, tipping it up, gently wiped off the rest of the ketchup with his napkin.

"I'm so embarrassed!" I said.

"You shouldn't be. Ketchup looks good on you."

Our eyes met, and my heart gave a funny little leap. *It would be a pity to ruin everything by making my confession now*, I thought. I could get used to this kind of treatment.

By the time we returned to the Coliseum at one o'clock, I was filled with a warm, fuzzy glow.

"Thank you, Spencer," I said as he drove the Volkswagen up to the backstage door. "I can't remember when I've had such a great time."

"Does that mean you'll have lunch with me again tomorrow?" he asked.

"Tomorrow?" I asked, surprised.

"Yeah, tomorrow," he said.

"I don't want to monopolize all your time . . ." I said, tentatively.

"That's funny. I don't feel the least bit guilty about monopolizing all of yours," he retorted. "You'll be going back to Florida in a couple of weeks, and I intend to make good use of the time we've got together. Tomorrow I thought we might take the streetcar tour of the historic district, if you'd like."

"Okay, if you're sure," I said hesitantly.

"Positive. Tomorrow, then? Same time, same place?"

I knew I shouldn't accept another date under false pretenses, but I just couldn't resist. "I'll be here," I said.

I had heard of whirlwind romances, but I had never experienced one until now. I went through the rest of the day in a daze. When Kim called me that night, I was still floating on a fluffy pink cloud.

"All right, Wendy, tell me everything!" Kim demanded eagerly, not even taking time to say hello. "How was your date with Spencer Phyffe?"

I sighed. "It was wonderful," I told her.

"So what did he say when you told him?"

My cloud evaporated, and I fell abruptly to earth. "I couldn't tell him, Kim. Everything was so perfect, and I didn't want anything to spoil it. I just *couldn't*."

After a pause, Kim said, "Oh, well, I guess you don't have to spill your guts on the first date."

"What about the second?" I asked.

"What do you mean?"

"We have another lunch date for tomorrow. Spencer's taking me on a tour of the historic district."

"But Wendy, you don't *need* a tour," Kim pointed out. "You've lived here all your life."

"Yeah, but *he* doesn't know that."

"Just how long do you plan to keep this up, anyway?"

"Oh, not much longer," I told her. "When the time is right, I'll know it, and then I'll tell him who I really am."

"You're afraid he'll ditch you if he finds out, aren't you?" Kim said.

"Of course not!" I said a little too hotly. "Spencer's not like that at all!"

"All right, all right! Chill out! So where did he take you for lunch?"

"We ate hamburgers in the park." I smiled at the memory.

"You're really hung up on this guy, aren't you?" Kim asked, suddenly serious.

"Well, I wouldn't say I'm in love, but I'm very seriously in like," I admitted.

"I guess you know what you're doing," Kim said doubtfully, "but I can't help having a funny feeling about this whole business. I just hope you don't end up getting hurt."

# Four

It was easy to disregard Kim's warning; after all, she'd done plenty of crazy things to get Dave's attention. I lay awake for a long time that night, thinking about Spencer. Spencer didn't have to throw a lot of his money around to make a good impression on me. Surely a guy with that kind of self-assurance wouldn't care whether he was dating a beauty queen or a seamstress. *I'll tell him tomorrow,* I thought. I closed my eyes and lay there in the dark, picturing the scene.

"Spencer," I would say, "I have a confession to make. I'm not really Clarissa Devoe, Florida's Teen Beauty. I'm Wendy Miller, a pageant seamstress."

"It doesn't matter to me who you are," he would say. "I love you just the same."

Then he would take me in his arms and bend his head to mine, and—

BRRRINNNNG!

When had I fallen asleep? *Drat that alarm clock*, I thought sleepily, rolling over to turn it off.

Even though my dream had been rudely interrupted, part of it lingered with me throughout the morning. As I waited on the contestants, I felt a little like Cinderella, knowing that my prince was out there some- where, and he would be waiting for me at noon. By midmorning I had caught up on all my work, and there was nothing left to do but watch the clock and listen to Mrs. Crow- ley and Mrs. Evans discuss somebody's gall- bladder surgery. At eleven-thirty, I was rescued by Sonya Langley, Ohio's Teen Beauty.

"Wendy, do you have a minute?" she asked, entering the sewing room.

"Sure," I said, glad to get away from gall-bladders. "What do you need?"

"I changed my mind about which shoes to wear for the talent competition," she explained. "I had a pair dyed to match my gown, but under the floodlights, the colors clash. These shoes look better, but they have lower heels, so now my dress drags on the ground."

"I can raise the hem for you, but you'll need to try it on with the shoes so I can pin it up," I said.

Sonya left the room and returned a few minutes later wearing her gown and the shoes. I stuck some straight pins into the hem of my shirt, and sat down on the floor at her feet.

"You'll be playing the piano for your talent, won't you?" I asked, turning up the hem and marking it with a pin.

"Uh-huh. And what a piano! Have you seen it?"

"I was here the day they brought it in," I replied, thinking of my first formal meeting with Spencer.

I was just putting the last pin in Sonya's

39

dress when I heard the voice of one of the other girls out in the hall.

"Clarissa! Has anybody seen Clarissa Devoe?"

"Here I am," Clarissa called from the cubicle that served as her dressing room. "What is it?"

"There's some guy at the back door asking for you. He says his name is Spencer."

*Ouch!* I jabbed a pin into my thumb.

"Spencer?" Clarissa asked. "I don't know anybody named Spencer."

"Boy, I wish I did!" the first girl said. "This guy is *cute!*"

"I'll be right down," Clarissa said.

Ignoring the pain in my thumb, I scrambled to my feet. "He's probably just some autograph hunter," I said, trying to sound casual. Then I yelled, "I'll take care of it, Clarissa."

"Would you, Wendy? Thanks," Clarissa called back.

I flew down the hall and flung open the backstage door. Sure enough, there stood Spencer.

"Hi," he said. "Ready to go?"

"Not just yet," I answered. "I'm—uh—right in the middle of a fitting. Give me five minutes, and I'll be right with you."

I shut the door quickly and hurried back to Clarissa's dressing room.

"It was nothing, Clarissa," I said airily. "Just a mix-up." Then I dashed into the sewing room. "Sonya, if you'll leave that dress here, I should have it finished this afternoon."

After she had gone, I grabbed my purse, stopped in the restroom just long enough to run a brush through my hair, and joined Spencer.

"Sorry for the delay," I said as we climbed into the flaming yellow VW. "Things are getting crazy around here, the closer we get to the big day."

"How much longer is it, anyway?" Spencer asked.

"Two weeks from tomorrow." A horrible thought occurred to me. "Are you planning to come?"

"Are you kidding? Do you know what tickets to that thing cost?"

"No," I confessed.

"It's fifty dollars for a seat in the stratosphere—a lot more than that, if you want to be close enough to actually see anything. I'll just watch it on TV," Spencer said.

I was puzzled by his remark. He *could* afford it, after all. But then again, this was another example of how down-to-earth Spencer was.

"Do you mind if I ask you a personal question?" Spencer was asking me when I snapped out of my thoughts.

"Depends on what it is," I said lightly, but all my nerves switched over to red alert.

"Why do you have all those pins stuck in your shirt?"

I looked down. Sure enough, three pins were left over from my fitting with Sonya. In my haste, I had forgotten to remove them.

"I was helping one of the girls with her hem," I explained as I took out the pins and dropped them into my purse.

Spencer gave me a skeptical smile. "Helping the competition? Sure you weren't planning a little sabotage?"

"Oh, no," I said. "We help each other out all the time." Yeah, right. I helped them compete for a crown, a title, and a college scholarship, and they helped *me* earn minimum wage for three weeks. It wasn't exactly an even trade.

Spotting a brown paper bag on the dashboard, I took the opportunity to change the subject. "What's in here?" I asked.

"Junk food," Spencer said cheerfully. "I forgot to warn you yesterday, but the tour runs about forty-five minutes. We won't have time for a real meal, so I bought enough popcorn and peanuts to feed an army. I hope you don't mind."

How could I possibly mind? I couldn't think about food when Spencer was around, anyway. I assured him that popcorn and peanuts were just fine with me.

We reached the streetcar just as it began to load. By the time Spencer parked the car and we scrambled aboard, all the best seats were taken. We finally squeezed into a spot in the back of the car, but our view was partially blocked by a very fat woman wearing a large-brimmed hat. Suddenly Spencer leapt up.

"I'll tell you what," he said. "I'll bet if the tour guide knew he had a real live Teen

Beauty on board, he'd put us up front. I'll be right back!"

"No!" I cried, grabbing his sleeve. "This seat is fine, Spencer, really it is. I don't want to inconvenience anybody."

Spencer reluctantly sat back down beside me. "You know," he said, "I think I owe beauty queens everywhere an apology. Before I met you, I'd always figured they were a bunch of self-absorbed prima donnas."

He had just described Clarissa perfectly, but I felt obligated to defend Jillian and Sonya and some of the others. "Oh, a few are like that, but most of them are really nice," I told him.

He smiled down at me. "I'm finding that out. That's what I like about you. You're *real*."

I cringed inside. If he only knew! But this was obviously not a good time for true confessions. It was a relief when the streetcar lurched forward and the tour guide began his opening remarks. From our seat at the rear, he was hard to understand, so Spencer gave me his own description of the district's stately old homes. Of course, the tour didn't

44

show me anything I hadn't already seen a dozen times, but somehow that didn't matter. When I was with Spencer, everything was new and exciting, as if I were seeing it all for the first time.

"There's Camellia House," he said, pointing to a beautiful white house on our left. "It was built in the 1840s and completely restored just a few years ago. That's where they're holding the Teen Beauty Ball the night before the pageant."

I leaned to the side, trying to get the best view around the lady's hat. I had seen Camellia House many times, although I had never been inside. It was a huge, two-story building with imposing white columns. I could picture girls in elegant ball gowns and guys in tuxedos strolling up and down its wide veranda.

"I can't imagine what it must be like, going to a function like that," I said softly, hardly realizing that I had spoken my thoughts aloud.

"Give yourself a couple of weeks, and you won't have to imagine it."

Spencer's remark brought me back to the

present. This was a perfect opportunity to tell him that I wouldn't be attending the ball, and why, but I didn't want to explain everything on a crowded streetcar. Or maybe the streetcar was just a good excuse for postponing what I really didn't want to do in the first place. At any rate, I said nothing. At last the tour ended, and Spencer drove me back to the Coliseum.

"Wait a minute," he said as I got out of the car. "How about having dinner with me tomorrow night?"

"I'd like that," I said, and I meant it.

"Great! Where did you say you were staying?"

"Five fifty-seven Woodland Drive," I said, then added quickly, "but you don't have to pick me up. I can meet you there."

Spencer grinned. "Meet me where? We haven't even decided on a restaurant."

"Well, let's pick one now, and I'll meet you there tomorrow night."

"No way!" he said firmly. "I'm not going to let you wander around a strange town looking for me. I'll pick you up at six."

"I—I don't think that would be a good idea," I mumbled.

Spencer's eyebrows drew together in a puzzled frown. "Why not?"

"Well, because—because—the Millers' house is under quarantine!" I said, offering the first excuse that popped into my head.

"Is somebody sick?"

I nodded. "Both of them. Smallpox."

"I thought nobody got smallpox anymore," Spencer said.

"Well, the Millers did," I said with a helpless shrug. Just my luck to choose a disease that no longer existed!

"Are you sure it's safe for you to be staying there?" Spencer asked, his voice filled with concern.

"Well, it was too late to make other arrangements, and besides, I've had a smallpox shot."

Spencer's brow cleared. "Then that settles it! I've had one, too."

"Oh," I said, wracking my brain for some other reason to keep him from coming. "There's something else. The Millers, they—

they have this really ferocious attack dog, and it—"

"Clarissa, are you trying to get rid of me?" Spencer asked.

"Of course not!" I said quickly. "It's just that—"

"Then never let it be said that a Phyffe was afraid of man, beast, pestilence, or plague!" Spencer declared melodramatically. "I laugh at danger! I scoff at fear! I'll pick you up tomorrow at six—no more arguments!"

He drove away before I could protest, leaving me to face another major hurdle. What were my parents going to say when a boy turned up on their doorstep asking for Clarissa Devoe?

# Five

"Imagine you—Florida's Teen Beauty," I told my reflection sternly, studying it critically in my bedroom mirror. I was pretty enough, I guess, in an ordinary sort of way—brown hair, brown eyes, and fair skin that had hardly seen the sun since school let out. But I was certainly no match for the real Clarissa. I sighed and turned to leave my room. As I started slowly down the stairs I tried to summon all of my courage. It was time to face Mom and Dad, and I wasn't looking forward to it.

"Well, don't you look lovely," Mom said, looking up from the television as I entered the room.

I surprised her by sitting down on the arm of her chair and giving her an impulsive hug. "Thanks, Mom. I needed that!"

"Still, it's not often that you dress up so for a date. This boy must really be special."

"Yeah, he is," I answered, nervously smoothing the collar of my navy-and-white sailor dress.

"We're looking forward to meeting him," Mom went on.

"Oh, you don't have to if you don't want to," I said, a little too quickly.

"Of course we want to," Dad said. "Why shouldn't we want to meet a young man with the good taste to date our daughter?"

"Well—uh—the thing is, he doesn't exactly *know* that I'm your daughter," I floundered. "I mean, when he gets here, he won't know that you're my parents."

Dad frowned. "Who will he think we are, if not your parents?"

I knew it wouldn't be easy, but this was

turning out to be even harder than I'd thought. Maybe Mom and Dad would be more understanding if I pointed out the humor in the situation.

"He'll think you're my lost family," I said with a nervous giggle. "He thinks I'm Florida's Teen Beauty. Isn't that hysterical?"

Mom and Dad were not amused. "And just how did he get that impression?" Mom asked, her voice dangerously calm.

So much for humor. I took a deep breath and launched into my explanation. I told them the whole story, and finished by saying, ". . . and so he thinks I'm Clarissa Devoe. I never meant to lie about it—it just sort of *happened*! And now I don't know what to do about it."

There was a long silence. Finally, Mom said, "When did you say you met this boy?"

"Tuesday," I mumbled.

Dad lost his temper. "Wendy Miller, do you mean you've let this go on for *four whole days*?"

Before I could try to defend myself, I heard the sound of a car outside.

51

I leapt to my feet. "He's here! Mom—Dad—*please* don't say anything embarrassing! I'll straighten out the whole mess, I promise!"

Before either of them could respond, the doorbell rang, and I ran to let Spencer in. Trembling inwardly, I introduced my parents as Mr. and Mrs. Miller.

"It must be interesting, hosting one of the Teen Beauty contestants for three weeks," Spencer remarked as he shook hands with Dad.

"Oh, 'interesting' doesn't begin to describe it," Dad said. "She's just like one of the family."

"Won't you sit down, Spencer?" Mom asked politely.

I followed Spencer to the couch, but just as we sat down, I saw disaster staring at me from the opposite side of the room. There on top of the television set was the framed family photo we'd had taken last spring! Leaping up from the couch, I dashed across the room and planted myself directly in front of the television.

"Don't you want to sit down?" Spencer asked.

"*No!* I mean, no," I said, more calmly this time. "I'd rather stand."

"Well, then, would you mind moving to one side or the other?" Dad suggested. "I'm trying to watch the news on TV."

"Don't you find the newspaper *much* more informative?" I said desperately.

At that moment Suzy, Mom's tiny Chihuahua, came trotting into the room. The little dog headed for the couch and began to sniff at Spencer curiously. Spencer held out his hand, and Suzy began to lick it with enthusiasm. I seized the opportunity to turn the photo facedown on top of the television set.

Spencer grinned up at me. "Is this the attack dog that was supposed to eat me alive?"

Mom came swiftly to her pet's defense. "Why, Suzy has never bitten anyone in her life, have you, Suzy girl?"

"I guess it's nice to have a pet around when you can't have visitors," Spencer remarked. I stifled a groan. I'd completely forgotten about the smallpox story!

"We can't have visitors?" Mom asked, confused.

"Because of the quarantine," Spencer replied.

"Quarantine?" Mom echoed. She was completely at a loss. "Has someone been sick?"

"Just look at the time!" I interrupted loudly. "I guess we'd better be going, right, Spencer?" As I dragged him out the door, I whispered, "It's the medication. It makes them forgetful sometimes."

It was a relief to get out of the house, but I was a little surprised to see the same yellow Volkswagen sitting in the driveway.

"Still no Jag?" I asked as Spencer opened the car door for me.

"No," he said, laughing. "I'm afraid I'll be waiting for it a long time. I hope you like Italian food. I thought we might go to Angelo's."

I had never been to Angelo's before, so I didn't have to pretend ignorance. We both ordered the fettucine Alfredo, and it was delicious. Spencer attacked his plate with such enthusiasm that I wondered how he managed to stay so slim.

"If I ate like that, I'd weigh two hundred pounds," I remarked.

"Oh, I work most of it off," he said with a grin.

"Doing what?" I could just picture him playing polo or swimming laps in his family's private pool.

"Well, I guess it's from moving and shaking all day," he answered.

I wasn't sure what he meant, so all I said was, "I'm impressed!"

"You shouldn't be, really. It's pretty sporadic work, but it pays pretty well. And like my dad says, it keeps me out of trouble."

I wanted to hear more about Spencer's job, but before I could ask him any questions, the waitress came to refill our water glasses.

"I'm glad to see that you eat real food," Spencer told me as the waitress reached 'for my empty glass. "I thought all beauty queens lived on lettuce and cottage cheese."

"To tell you the truth, I hate cottage cheese," I confessed. Still, I did have a role to play, so when the dessert cart came around, I took one longing glance at the chocolate cheesecake before deciding on fresh fruit. The rest of the meal passed without incident—until we were ready to leave. Just as I was getting up from my chair, a boy who was passing by our table bumped into me.

"Hey, I'm sorry," he said, taking a quick step backward. "I guess I'd better watch where I'm going."

To my horror, I found myself looking up into a familiar face. I couldn't remember his name, but I knew him from somewhere— maybe school? In any case, I hoped and prayed that he wouldn't remember me, but I saw recognition dawn in his eyes.

"Say, don't I know you?" he asked.

"I—I don't think so," I stammered. "You must have me confused with someone else."

"Are you sure?" he persisted. "You look so familiar. I'm positive I've met you before."

"I'm sorry," I said coolly.

"I remember now!" he said, snapping his fingers. "You're—"

"No, I'm not," I cut in, no longer even trying to be polite.

He stared at me. "But—"

"Look, is something wrong with your hearing?" Spencer said, standing up. "Even if you *had* met Clarissa before, it's obvious you didn't make much of an impression. So maybe you'd better drop it, okay?"

The poor boy stepped away, muttering incoherent apologies, as Spencer took me by the arm and escorted me out of the restaurant.

"Thanks," I murmured to Spencer as soon as we got into his car. "I was beginning to wonder how I was ever going to get rid of that guy."

"No problem," he said, taking my hand and giving it a reassuring squeeze. "I guess that's the price you pay for being a beauty queen. I would have thought you'd be used to it by this time."

"Oh, it happens everywhere I go," I said in a bored, beauty-queen voice. "Most of them aren't that persistent, though."

"Most of them probably have a better line, too. That haven't-I-met-you-before routine is as old as they get."

"I'm sure you, on the other hand, would have thought of a terrific one," I said, giving him a mischievous smile.

"Who, me? I don't use lines! I distinctly remember bowling you over with my musical genius."

"Oh, is that what you call it?" I teased.

"Hey, it did the trick, didn't it?" he retorted. "Speaking of music, how is our piano holding up?"

"It's being kept pretty busy," I told him. "Since the preliminaries start on Monday, everybody wants a chance to practice."

"So the pageant starts Monday? I thought it was going to be on TV a week from Friday."

"It is. But that will be the finals. There are two weeks of preliminary competition."

"I guess things must stay pretty busy around there, huh?" Spencer said.

"You better believe it! Last week the electricians were installing the special lighting and sound equipment. And next week the place will be crawling with photographers and television news crews."

Spencer glanced over at me and smiled. "I'll have to remember to watch the news every night."

I made a mental note to avoid anything even remotely resembling a TV camera, but I could hardly expect the real Clarissa to do the same.

Soon we reached my house. Spencer took my arm as we mounted the steps onto the porch. When we reached the front door, he drew me close, taking both my hands in his.

"Thank you for dinner," I told him, gazing up into his bright blue eyes. "Everything was just perfect."

"No, not quite," he said. "There's still one thing missing."

"What?"

For an answer, Spencer bent his head and kissed me gently on the lips. "That," he murmured.

Hearing no argument from me, he kissed me again, more thoroughly this time. For a moment, it was just like a dream. Then reality reared its ugly head as Spencer whispered soft and low into my ear, "You're really a special girl, Clarissa."

He might as well have thrown a bucket of cold water in my face. It was terrible to hear myself called by someone else's name at such a romantic moment.

Without thinking, I blurted out, "Please—

call me Wendy. All my friends do. It's my real name. Clarissa is my middle name—I only use it for pageants."

"Wendy," Spencer repeated. "It suits you better than Clarissa, I think. Well, Wendy, would you like to go out again tomorrow night?"

I was about to say "Of course," but then I remembered the schedule. "I'd like to, but I can't. We—all the Teen Beauties—are supposed to visit the children's wards of the local hospitals tomorrow. It'll probably be an all-day thing."

"Well, I guess I don't mind giving you up to some sick kids for one day," Spencer said reluctantly. "Are you free for lunch next Monday, then?"

"Monday sounds fine," I said, then realized my mistake. "Wait a minute, though. Contestants from Alabama through Montana have their interviews on Monday. Heaven only knows when I'll get a chance to eat lunch."

"Interviews, huh? Are you nervous?" Spencer asked.

"Terrified," I answered in perfect truth.

After he had gone, I slowly climbed the stairs to my room, where I found Mom sitting on the bed waiting for me. I expected her to be angry, but all she said was, "How was your evening, honey?"

"It was great," I said dreamily. And it had been, too. Granted, there had been a few close calls, but the good parts more than made up for the bad.

"So you told him the truth?" Mom went on.

Avoiding her eyes, I shook my head sadly. "I'm sorry, Mom."

My mother frowned, obviously exasperated. "Wendy, you don't have to pretend to be someone else just to impress a boy!"

"But Mom, Spencer's not 'just a boy!' He's different from any guy I've ever known, and he treats me like I'm really special."

"But Wendy, honey, you *are* special!" Mom insisted.

"No, I'm not! I'm not beautiful, or poised, or talented, like all the Teen Beauties."

"You don't have to be a beauty queen to be somebody special, you know," Mom said quietly.

"To you and Dad, maybe, but—"

"To lots of people. What about Kevin Hanks? He'd ask you out in a minute, if you'd just act a little bit interested."

"Kevin's okay, but he's no Spencer Phyffe," I said.

"Say what you will about Kevin. But if you were dating him, you wouldn't have to wonder if he was ashamed to be seen with you."

That really hurt. "Spencer wouldn't be ashamed to be seen with me!" I protested hotly.

"If you're so sure of that, why haven't you told him who you are?" Mom asked.

Unable to answer, I just stared down at the quilted bedspread.

"Wendy, I think you're letting yourself in for more grief than you can imagine," Mom went on. "I know it's hard, when you've found somebody you like a lot, to think he might not be as wonderful as you want him to be. But if he isn't, wouldn't it be better to find out now, before you get too emotionally involved?" She leaned forward and kissed me on the forehead. "Think about it, honey. I'm sure you'll see what I mean."

I saw what she meant, all right. But what Mom didn't know—what I couldn't possibly tell her—was that her advice came too late. I was already too emotionally involved.

# Six

I'm not sure if Monday was really a lousy day, or if it only seemed that way compared to the week before. Now that the Teen Beauty competition was actually underway, the seamstresses' workload was doubled, and the added pressure began to grate on everyone's nerves. Added to that were the TV camera crews that lurked around every corner, keeping me constantly on guard to avoid appearing on the six o'clock news.

And worst of all, after all those romantic lunches with Spencer, I was left to eat alone.

Kim couldn't join me, since she was being sent to the airport to meet the emcee of the pageant.

After grabbing a hamburger at the Hut, I returned to the Coliseum well before the end of my lunch hour, hoping to get a head start on the afternoon's work. I parked my car and had just reached the backstage door when a delivery van marked Betty's Blossom Shop drew up beside me.

"Excuse me, miss," the driver called, "are you with the America's Teen Beauty Pageant?"

"Yes, I am," I answered.

"I have a delivery for one of the contestants. Can you take it to her?"

"Sure."

It wasn't unusual for the girls to receive flowers or even balloons from home. Most of their families wouldn't be flying in until next week, and some of the girls had boyfriends who couldn't make the trip at all. I waited as the driver disappeared into the rear of the van and soon emerged holding a long white box.

"I'll need you to sign here," he said, offering me a pencil and a clipboard. "It's for a Clarissa Devoe."

I signed along the dotted line and returned the clipboard to the driver.

I found Clarissa sitting in front of the mirror in her dressing room while her makeup artist, Rob, and her hairdresser, Sally, bustled about, preparing Clarissa for her two o'clock interview.

"—And now my dress smells like hospital disinfectant," Clarissa was complaining. "Honestly, why we had to waste a whole day with a bunch of sick kids is beyond me!"

"Clarissa, have you got a minute?" I asked, tapping lightly on the open door. "Some flowers just came for you."

"Sure," Clarissa answered.

I came inside, handed her the box, and watched as she removed the lid. Inside lay a single long-stemmed red rose nestled in a bed of greenery and baby's breath.

"Oh, how lovely," Sally said. "Who's it from?"

"Let's see . . ." Clarissa opened the card

and read it aloud. " 'Knock 'em dead. Spencer.' "

My eyes flew wide open. "Did you say *Spencer*?"

"That's what it says," Clarissa said, frowning thoughtfully at the card.

"Didn't somebody named Spencer try to get in to see you last week?" Rob asked.

"Sounds like you've picked up a secret admirer," Sally said, twirling a strand of Clarissa's long hair around a curling iron.

"Let me put that in water for you," I said, trying to hide my eagerness. I usually resented doing favors for Clarissa, but at that moment I would have done anything to spend just a moment alone with *my* rose. And it *was* mine!

I went to the sewing room and found an empty Coke bottle, then took it to the rest room and filled it with water. I gently slid the slender stem into the narrow neck of the bottle.

When I returned to the dressing room, Clarissa and the others were talking about the mysterious Spencer.

"Maybe he saw you at the charity luncheon

or the Scenic Gardens tour, and fell in love at first sight," Sally suggested.

"Or maybe he's a psycho who has a fatal attraction for you," said Rob with a manic leer.

Clarissa shuddered. "Do you really think so?" she asked, wide-eyed with apprehension.

"Could be. They made a movie about that sort of thing, you know. I'd watch out if I were you."

" 'Knock 'em dead. Spencer,' " Clarissa said, reading the card once more. "It *does* have a sort of sinister ring to it, now that you mention it."

I choked back a giggle as I placed the bottle on the dressing table. I couldn't help wondering what Clarissa would say if she knew that the rose had come from the son of one of Bellevue's wealthiest citizens, and that the 'fatal attraction' wasn't directed at her—but at a lowly seamstress instead!

That night, I called Kim and told her all about it. We had a good laugh at Clarissa's expense, and then Kim asked a question that was no laughing matter.

"So what are you going to do now, Wendy?"

I took a deep breath. "I have to tell him the truth."

"He might not be too thrilled to find out that the flower he ordered for you went to a complete stranger," Kim pointed out.

"I've thought of that, believe me! And that's only one of the reasons why I owe it to Spencer to be honest with him."

But when I met Spencer at Portofino Pizza for lunch the next day, he was so nice to "Clarissa the beauty queen" that I couldn't help wondering what sort of treatment "Wendy the seamstress" would get. Maybe Mom was right—maybe he wasn't as wonderful as I thought he was. And maybe I really didn't want to know.

Spencer ordered a pizza, and I decided to put off my confession until our order came. If Spencer had his hands full of pizza, at least he couldn't do anything drastic—like grab me by the throat and strangle me. Pizzas usually seem to take forever, but our order was ready all too soon. I couldn't stall any longer, so I picked up a slice and cautiously began.

"Spencer, about the rose you sent—"

"Oh, did you get it?" He sounded almost surprised.

"Yes. It came yesterday, just after lunch."

Something in my tone of voice or facial expression must have puzzled him. "There was nothing wrong with it, was there?" Spencer asked. "I specifically asked for—"

"Oh no, no! It's just beautiful," I assured him quickly. "It's just that . . ."

"Just that what?"

"Just that—it was awfully sweet of you," I said, chickening out. "Thanks so much."

He smiled. "Well, I thought you might have had a tough day, with the interviews and all. How did it go, anyway?"

"Oh, fine," I mumbled.

"What did they ask you about?"

"Uh—environmental issues, mostly," I said, remembering bits of conversation I had heard between several of the contestants.

Spencer let out a low whistle. "Pretty deep stuff. How did you answer?"

"Oh, please!" I begged, rolling my eyes. "Don't make me go through all that again!"

Spencer polished off his first slice of pizza and reached for a second. "I've never paid much attention to the pageant before, but I've been doing my homework this year," he said. "I didn't know that the interviews count for forty percent of the total score."

"Where did you learn that?" I asked.

"From the newspaper. I learned quite a bit about you, too."

I almost choked on my pizza. "Like what?"

"Oh, like that you want to go to the University of Miami, and that you plan to be an actress."

An actress? Fine for Clarissa, maybe, but not for me. I'd had enough acting lately to last me a lifetime!

"The Sunday paper had a profile of each contestant," Spencer went on.

How on earth had I managed to miss that? "I see. And was there a picture of—me—in the paper?"

"No, just a short paragraph. But I wonder how they ever got the idea that you have blue eyes."

I shrugged, trying to seem nonchalant. "If you had to interview fifty-two teenage girls, I guess after a while they'd all start to look alike."

"I don't know about that," Spencer said, grinning as he reached for a third slice of pizza. "I'd remember *you*."

"I just hope the judges feel the same way," I said with my best beauty-queen smile, and seized the opportunity to change the subject.

# Seven

Kim came over to my house that night, and in the privacy of my bedroom, I told her all about the close call I'd had that afternoon.

"You mean you didn't tell him after all?" she asked, obviously surprised and disappointed.

"I tried, Kim! I really tried. But when a guy cares enough to send one perfect rose, it just seems like a lousy way to thank him."

Kim still looked unconvinced, but before she could answer, Mom tapped on the door. "Telephone call for you, Wendy," she said.

"Boy or girl?" I asked.

"Boy. I think it's Spencer. And I noticed he asked for *Wendy*," she added, her voice warm with approval. "I knew you would do the right thing, honey. I'm proud of you."

I gave her a weak smile, unable to admit that I still hadn't told Spencer the truth.

I ran down the hall and picked up the extension in Mom and Dad's bedroom. But the caller wasn't Spencer at all. It was Kevin Hanks, who wanted to know if I could go out with him Saturday night. I declined as politely as possible.

"One thing you have to say for Kevin," I said to Kim as I walked back into my room. "He doesn't give up easily."

"Kevin's a nice guy," Kim said. "Maybe you should go out with him just this once, to reward him for being so persistent."

I shook my head. "Sorry. Persistence is *not* one of the things I'm looking for in a relationship."

"Neither is honesty, apparently," Kim said dryly.

"Kim, you're not being fair!" I hesitated for a moment, then added, "You know, in some ways, I wish Spencer was a little more like Kevin."

She stared at me. "*This* is news! In what way?"

"Well, I know most girls would kill or die to go out with a guy like Spencer, but sometimes I wish he were a little more—average. If only he wasn't so rich, I wouldn't worry so much about telling him who I am. In fact, I probably wouldn't have pulled such a stupid stunt in the first place."

" 'Oh, what a tangled web we weave, when first we practice to deceive!' " Kim said darkly.

*You can say that again,* I thought. Over the last week, I'd certainly found it to be true. What had begun as a simple case of mistaken identity had snowballed completely out of control. And the threat of exposure was never far away. Every time I picked up a newspaper or turned on the television, I was reminded of just how close I stood to the brink of disaster.

Then on Friday night, it happened. I was sitting on the couch watching the six o'clock news when suddenly, there in living color was the real Clarissa Devoe. Horrified, I sat bolt upright, as a reporter asked Clarissa her impressions of the national competition. A caption appeared on the screen, identifying her as Clarissa Devoe, Florida's Teen Beauty.

"I'm dead," I groaned. "If Spencer sees this, I'm dead!"

"I wouldn't worry about it if I were you," Kim told me a few minutes later, when I phoned to tell her of this latest crisis. "I don't think a guy like Spencer Phyffe spends much time sitting around watching TV. He's probably off escorting some gorgeous deb to a ritzy society party or something."

"If that's your way of cheering me up, I don't think much of it!" I retorted.

Still, Spencer out with another girl was a more comforting thought than Spencer at home watching television. At any rate, I wouldn't have to wait long to find out, since we had a date for the very next night.

When I met him at the door on Saturday night, I was a nervous wreck. Spencer seemed to give me such a measuring look that I was sure he had found me out. But the next instant, that look was gone. Had it really been there at all, I wondered, or was my guilty conscience making me imagine things?

"Just think, Wendy," Spencer said as we drove to the theater. "By this time next week, it'll all be over."

With a sinking heart, I realized he was right. It *would* be all over between him and me.

"I've been thinking," he continued. "My folks are planning a trip to Florida in August. Maybe I could come with them and visit you."

"No!" I said quickly. "I—I mean, I don't think that's a good idea. You see, I—I won't be there myself."

*That's it*, my conscience urged. *Go ahead—tell him! This thing has gone on long enough.*

"Oh, really?" Spencer asked, raising his eyebrows in surprise. "Where will you be?"

"Well—uh—I'll be making personal appearances all over the state. No matter what happens in the finals, I still have my state title, you know."

So much for my conscience.

Spencer shrugged. "Well, it was just a

thought. What sort of prizes do you win at the state level, anyway?"

I didn't have the foggiest idea. "I've been living and breathing pageant for the last two weeks," I pleaded. "Can't we talk about something else?"

Spencer changed the subject readily enough, but my troubles weren't over yet. As soon as we were seated in the theater, I spotted a group of kids from my school sitting several rows in front of us. They had their backs to us, but I instinctively slid down lower in my seat.

"Is anything wrong?" Spencer asked.

"Oh, no," I assured him. "I'm just getting comfortable."

Fat chance! I was so frantically juggling my dual identities that sometimes I wondered if I would ever be comfortable again. But then as the theater lights went down, Spencer reached over and took my hand, and I decided to enjoy the moment while it lasted.

But I couldn't help thinking about what Spencer had said earlier. In less than a week the pageant would be over, and so would our brief romance. The real Clarissa Devoe would return to Florida, and Wendy Miller would probably never see Spencer Phyffe again. I was bound to lose in the end.

On the other hand, if I told Spencer the truth tonight—then what? I cast a sideways glance at his handsome profile, wondering for the millionth time if it would really matter to him that I wasn't a beauty queen. True, he didn't act like a snob, but maybe that was only because he thought I was glamorous and special.

Sensing my eyes on him, Spencer turned and gave me a tender smile. As I returned his smile, I knew I couldn't risk losing him just yet.

# Eight

Monday morning got off to a rousing start when I heard a piercing scream from Clarissa's dressing room. The other seamstresses and I hurried down the corridor, followed by several of the contestants. I reached Clarissa's cubicle ahead of the pack, and found her in tears.

"I won't go!" she sobbed. "They can't make me go!"

"There, there, dear," Sally said, patting her on the back. "You don't really want to miss that lovely ball over a little thing like—"

Clarissa's blue eyes sparkled with anger. "A little thing? A *little* thing? I won't be humiliated this way!"

"What happened?" I asked the contestant standing next to me.

"It's Clarissa's ball gown," she whispered. "It's just like Miss Tennessee's. Same style, same color, same *everything*."

"Remember, Clarissa, there are fifty-two contestants," Sally pointed out reasonably. "Nobody will notice—"

*"Not notice?"* Clarissa shrieked. "I'm Florida's Teen Beauty! People are *supposed* to notice me!" It took the combined efforts of Sally, Mrs. Evans, Mrs. Crowley, and me to soothe Clarissa's ruffled feathers. By the time we hustled her out the door at nine-thirty, she was calmer, but still determined not to attend Thursday night's ball as a twin of Miss Tennessee.

The contestants had gone to an autograph signing, and the Coliseum backstage area was eerily quiet. But according to Mrs. Crowley and Mrs. Evans, who had both worked the pageant before, this was the calm before the storm. For the rest of the week, the contestants would be busy with rehearsals for the telecast of the finals. All the formal gowns would have to be cleaned and pressed, and of course Mrs. Crowley, Mrs. Evans, and I would be on hand Friday night to take care of last-minute emergencies. But for now, we were caught up with our work and had time on our hands.

The lighter work load gave me time to think, and my thoughts were far from pleasant. The pageant date was rapidly approaching, and I was going to have to decide whether to tell Spencer the truth, or let him find out, as he inevitably would, when the finals took place on Friday night.

I still hadn't made up my mind by the time I met Spencer at noon. We ate at the Bellevue mall, then spent the rest of my lunch break strolling hand in hand through the mall. When we reached the fountain at the center, Spencer dug a penny out of his pocket and handed it to me.

"Here," he said. "Make a wish."

What should I wish for? That Spencer knew who I really was and loved me anyway? That I had the courage to tell him? I knew that it would take more than wishing to solve my problem. Still, it was nice to think that there might be some magical way to make everything right, so I closed my eyes, whispered something that was half wish and half prayer, and threw the penny into the water. I opened my eyes just in time to see Spencer toss a penny in after mine.

"What did you wish for?" I asked him as we watched our pennies settle side by side on the bottom.

"I can't tell you," he said, taking my hand once more. "If I do, it won't come true."

"Do you think that stuff really works?"

"Who knows?" He shrugged. "Maybe, if you wish for something hard enough."

We walked on in silence for a while, until at last Spencer said, "Wendy, I'm afraid this will be our last lunch date. I'm going to be working a lot this week. Corporate Consolidated is moving to their new offices starting tomorrow."

"I read about that in the newspaper. Is that where you work?"

"Not exactly, but I'll be helping—" Spencer

stopped suddenly, and stared at something up ahead. "Well, look who's here!"

I followed his gaze toward the main entrance to the mall, and what I saw drained the blood from my face. A crowd was gathered around six long tables, and seated at the tables were fifty-two girls who had become very familiar to me over the last two weeks. I didn't know the autographing was at the mall.

"Let's get out of here," I said, tugging urgently at Spencer's sleeve.

"Don't you want to stop and say hello?"

"No, I just want to go!" I said desperately.

Spencer's eyes grew concerned as he looked at me. "Wendy, is something wrong?"

Thinking fast, I said, "Isn't it obvious? I—I forgot all about the autograph session!"

"Will you get in trouble?"

"Oh, boy, will I ever!" I said, telling the absolute truth.

"Come on, then. Maybe we can sneak out of here before anybody sees you."

But we were too late. At that moment Stephanie Graham, the contestant from Missouri, looked up and spotted me. Leaving her place at the table, she ran over to me.

"Wendy! I'm so glad you're here!" she exclaimed. "I've been wanting to talk to you about my formal. Last Friday during a rehearsal, I caught my heel in the hem and ripped it out. Do you think you could take care of it this afternoon?"

I wanted to dig a hole somewhere and crawl in it. "Sure, Stephanie," I mumbled. "No problem."

"Thanks! See you back at the Coliseum!" she said, and hurried back to her table.

"That's funny," Spencer remarked, giving me a curious look. "She didn't even seem to notice that you weren't signing autographs with the rest of them."

"Oh, well," I said. "I guess she was too concerned about her dress."

"That's another thing," Spencer said, frowning. "Why should you be expected to fix her dress?"

"Oh, I don't mind, really, I don't," I babbled. "Like I told you before, we all help each other out."

"Well, it looks as if you're being imposed

88

on. Next time, tell her she can fix her own dress. I don't understand why they didn't hire some menial to do things like that."

My heart dropped down to my shoes. There was no more question in my mind of whether or not to tell Spencer the truth. He had just given me a pretty good idea of what I could expect if he found out I was actually a "menial." As I had feared, Spencer really *was* a snob. But, snob or not, I was in love with him and there was absolutely nothing I could do about it.

The ride back to the Coliseum was a gloomy one for me. Neither of us said much, until Spencer parked the Volkswagen near the backstage door.

"Well, I guess this is it," I said, smiling feebly at him.

"No, not quite." Spencer reached into the chest pocket of his shirt. "I've got a surprise for you."

He pulled something out of his pocket and showed it to me. To my dismay, I realized that it was a ticket—not to Friday night's pageant, but to something infinitely worse.

"It's a ticket for the Teen Beauty Ball," he

explained. "I thought I could take you—if you don't mind having me for an escort."

"Of course I don't mind," I told him, hoping I sounded fairly normal. "It's just that—well, the senior cadets from Hickory Ridge Military Academy are supposed to escort the girls."

"Oh, I know they always invite the cadets so the girls will have plenty of guys to dance with, but they aren't paired up or anything like that," Spencer said cheerfully. "You can bring your own escort, as long as he's got a ticket—which I do."

It was crazy. It could never work! There was no way in the world that I could go to the ball with Spencer and not be found out. Besides, he was nothing but a snobby rich kid who looked down on "menials" like me. I'd probably be better off if I never saw him again.

"That's great," I said, to my amazement. "I can't think of anybody I'd rather go with!"

Spencer grinned. "Terrific! I'll give you a call and we'll work out all the details."

90

I had plenty of details to work out myself—like how I was going to get into that ball Thursday night. After he had gone, I dashed to the row of pay phones in the Coliseum lobby. I dug a quarter out of my purse, dropped it into the slot, and punched Kim's number at pageant headquarters.

"Kim!" I wailed. "You've got to help me! I need a ticket for the ball Thursday night. Are there any left?"

"Yes, but—Wendy, do you have any idea how much those things cost?"

"I don't know, and I don't care. I've just got to have one!"

"Okay, but I think you ought to know that even though the ball is billed as a big social event, it's really a fund-raiser. The money goes to the America's Teen Beauty Foundation for next year's scholarships."

"So how much are the tickets?" I asked.

"One hundred dollars each. Don't say I didn't warn you."

I couldn't say a word. I felt as if the ground were crumbling underneath my feet.

"Wendy? Are you still there?"

I gulped. "Yeah, I'm still here. Kim, can you—can you loan me some money, just until payday?"

"How much do you need?" she asked.

"I don't know," I said, doing a quick tally of my available funds. "Fifty dollars ought to do it."

"*Me?* Loan you *fifty dollars* on *my* salary? That's a laugh!"

"But Kim, you know Mom and Dad make me save half of every paycheck for college."

"Well, what about the other half?"

"I've already spent most of it," I confessed.

Kim sighed. "Wendy, I'd help you if I could, cross my heart. But my mom and dad docked my last paycheck to pay off the speeding ticket I got last week. I don't *have* fifty dollars. And why do you need a ticket to the ball, anyway?"

"Never mind," I said wearily. "Talk to you later."

*There's got to be some other way,* I thought as I made my way back to the sewing room. Lost in thought, I wandered past the sewing room and paused by Clarissa's dressing room. On impulse I went inside, sat on the stool, and stared into her mirror. My eyes focused on the reflection of something behind me. Hanging from a hook on the opposite wall was a long strip of white satin with the word "Florida" in black letters— Clarissa's extra sash! I rose slowly to my feet. Maybe—just maybe—there was a way, after all!

# Nine

I went over to Kim's house after work that day and told her what I planned to do. "Well?" I asked, waiting for her response. "What do you think?"

"If you *really* want to know what I think," Kim said honestly, "*I* think you've lost your mind! You'll never get away with pretending to be Florida's Teen Beauty at the ball!"

"Shhh!" I cast a furtive glance at the open door of Kim's bedroom. "Your mother might hear!"

"I wish she would! Maybe she could talk some sense into you!"

"I was hoping you might have a dress I could borrow," I continued.

"Wear the dress you wore to the junior prom," Kim said unsympathetically. "Just leave me out of this crazy scheme."

"I couldn't possibly wear that old thing," I wailed. "It looks so—so junior prom-ish."

"Then rent one," she replied, unmoved.

"If I could afford to rent a dress, I could afford to buy a ticket! Kim, I really need your help!" I begged.

"Wendy, do you honestly think you can pass yourself off as Clarissa Devoe right under the noses of the pageant officials?"

"Why not?" I asked, lifting my chin defiantly. "Clarissa won't be there, and except for taking a few publicity photos together, the pageant officials don't really have much contact with the contestants—you know that as well as I do. Who's going to notice if somebody else takes her place?"

"Yes, but what about the other fifty-one girls?" Kim asked. "They'll all know you're a fake."

"Not necessarily. Once I'm inside, I'll take off Clarissa's sash and blend into the crowd. How will anybody know I didn't have a ticket? Besides, the contestants are the guests of honor. They'll have more important things to do than spy on their seamstress."

"I'm not so sure," Kim said doubtfully. "It seems like an awful risk for a boy you probably won't even see again after this week."

"I know," I said, blinking back the tears that suddenly filled my eyes. "But it's *because* I might never see him again that I have to risk it."

"I feel like this whole thing is my fault, in a way," Kim said, sighing. "If I hadn't made such a big deal about the Phyffes and their money—"

I shook my head. "It's not because Spencer's family is rich. If he didn't have a dime, I'd still be crazy about him."

Slowly, Kim rose from where she was sitting on the foot of her bed. "In that case, I guess we'd better get started," she said reluctantly.

"Where are we going?" I asked, following her out of the room.

"To find Cinderella something to wear to the ball," she replied with a grin. "Since you're determined to go through with this, you might as well go down with all flags flying!"

Kim led the way to her sister's bedroom at the other end of the hall. "This is one of the advantages of having an older sister away at college," she said. "A whole closetful of clothes left unguarded. And I know just the dress for you!"

She flung open the closet door and took out a sapphire-blue gown with a voluminous skirt and big puffed sleeves. It was a dress fit for a queen—a beauty queen.

"This was for Karen's sorority formal last year," Kim said. "Well? What do you think?"

"Oh, Kim," I said, putting out a hand to touch the stiff taffeta. "It's perfect! Do you think it'll fit?"

"I don't see why not," she said. "You and Karen are just about the same size. And if it doesn't fit just right, what better person to alter it than Wendy Miller, seamstress to the stars? Just don't do anything to it that can't be undone later," she added.

"I won't," I promised as Kim draped the beautiful dress over my arms. "Oh, Kim, you're the grandest Fairy Godmother any Cinderella could ask for!"

"Don't mention it," Kim said modestly. "But you'll have to supply your own glass slippers. And one more thing—"

"What?"

"Good luck, Wendy. I have a feeling you're really going to need it!"

On Thursday night I reviewed my plan over and over as I dressed for the ball. Mom and Dad still thought I had told Spencer who I really was, and I didn't want to admit that I hadn't. So I'd managed to give them the impression—without saying it in so many words—that all the pageant employees had been invited to the ball. Over the last few weeks, I was ashamed to discover, I had become pretty good at bending the truth.

I picked up my dainty evening bag from the bed and looked inside. There, wound up into a tight roll, lay Clarissa's extra sash. I had smuggled it home from the Coliseum that very afternoon, and it was now ready and waiting for my big moment.

Satisfied, I closed the bag with a snap. I had to keep the sash hidden until I was out of the house. Of course, that would mean taking it out and putting it on in front of Spencer, but that shouldn't be a problem. Getting rid of it once I was safely through the door at the dance wouldn't be so easy, though.

When I finished dressing and turned to look at myself in the mirror, I could hardly believe my eyes. Was that really me? The dress, with its puffed sleeves, off-the-shoulder bodice and long, full skirt, made my waist look tiny, and the dark blue taffeta made my fair skin look positively luminous.

I turned my head slightly, and studied my elaborate new hairdo. Mom had arranged it for me high on the back of my head, with softly curling tendrils escaping to brush my cheeks. It was totally different from the simple style I usually wore, and I decided I loved it. It made me look glamorous and sophisticated—like Florida's Teen Beauty ought to look. My heart beat wildly at the thought. Spencer and I might not have a future together, but at least we would have one wonderful, unforgettable night. My last appearance as Clarissa Devoe would be my best.

When the doorbell rang ten minutes later, my taffeta skirts rustled as I went to the front door and opened it wide. There stood Spencer, looking so handsome and elegant in his black tuxedo that he took my breath away.

"You look great," I managed to whisper.

"I wish I could say the same for you, but I'm afraid 'great' doesn't even come close," he answered, gazing at me in awe.

Mom made all the usual remarks about how wonderful we looked, but when Dad suggested getting the camera and taking pictures, I knew it was time to go. We said our good-byes, and I hustled Spencer out of the house before my parents could betray me by behaving—well, like my parents. Once outside, I stopped short on the porch. Instead of the familiar Volkswagen, there in the driveway stood a sleek gray Lincoln.

"It's my parents' car," Spencer explained. "You didn't really think I was going to take you to a formal ball in my yellow bomb, did you?"

"I wouldn't have minded," I said softly, and I knew that it was true. I would gladly have gone anywhere with Spencer, in anything.

When we reached Camellia House, my earlier confidence began to fade. Suddenly I wasn't so sure my plan would work, but I had come too far to back down now. I took the sash out of my purse, unrolled it, and slipped it over my head.

"I didn't want it to get wrinkled," I explained to Spencer, conscious of his eyes on me.

As we made our way up the lamp-lit walkway, Spencer offered me his arm. Up ahead, another girl was escorted by a boy in a military dress uniform. I hung back a little, fearful of coming face-to-face with any of the contestants before I had a chance to dispose of my sash.

A uniformed security guard was stationed just outside the entrance, looking extremely menacing as he paced the wide veranda. He must have felt me looking at him, because at that moment he glanced up, and his eyes seemed to bore a hole straight through me. My heart leapt up into my throat. *He knows,* I thought. *He knows I'm a fake!* But in the next instant, he smiled, gave a little nod in our direction, and turned away. Still, I was relieved when we passed through the front doors, away from those watchful eyes.

Once inside, Spencer presented his ticket while I gazed at the surroundings. We had entered a large foyer, and a wide staircase covered with red carpet loomed up ahead. Glancing around, I noticed that the rest rooms were located at each end of the foyer. I made a mental note to duck into the ladies' room as soon as possible to remove my sash.

"May I take your purse?" a woman asked politely, holding out her hand for my evening bag. Instinctively, I clutched it tighter. The woman smiled, thinking she understood. "We'll lock it up for safekeeping," she explained.

I wasn't afraid of thieves—I didn't have anything worth stealing. But without my purse, where would I put the sash when I'd taken it off? Looking around me, I saw other new arrivals giving up their bags without protest. If I insisted on keeping mine, it might cause a scene, and the last thing I wanted was to call attention to myself. Reluctantly, I surrendered my bag.

"Thank you, sir," the ticket taker was saying to Spencer. "I hope you enjoy your evening."

We were in! My purse might have been impounded, but at least I had made it inside with no questions asked. Letting out a ragged breath, I took Spencer's arm once more, and together we mounted the red-carpeted stairs.

At the top of the stairs a second pair of double doors opened onto the ballroom. This would be a much harder test to pass, because just inside the ballroom, a number of pageant officials formed a receiving line. Spencer and I would have to go down the line and shake hands with each one of them. I gritted my teeth, plastered on my best beauty-queen smile, and plunged ahead.

Everything went well until halfway down the line when I shook hands with a lady who introduced herself as Mrs. Henry Forsythe,

the wife of the America's Teen Beauty Foundation president.

"So you're Florida's Teen Beauty," she said, squeezing my hand warmly. "I've been wanting to meet you. I'm a Florida girl myself."

"Oh? How nice," I said weakly.

"I do hope we'll get a chance to chat before the evening is over," she went on.

"That would be lovely," I answered, resolving to avoid her for the rest of the night.

It seemed like an eternity, but at last Spencer and I reached the end of the line, where I found myself facing Mr. Carrington, the pageant director—and my boss! I wanted to run and hide, but it was too late to turn back now. I looked him squarely in the eye as I held out my hand, hoping I could keep it from trembling.

"Good evening, Mr. Carrington," I said.

"Good evening," he said, taking my outstretched hand. "I hope you enjoy yourself tonight, Miss—uh . . ." He peered at my sash. "Miss Florida. You girls certainly deserve it after all the work you've put in."

He didn't recognize me! I don't know why I was so surprised—after all, Mr. Carrington couldn't be expected to know every girl by name. As for me, I certainly looked different from the girl he had chewed out just a couple of weeks ago for playing the Phyffes' piano. Mr. Carrington released my hand and turned to Spencer.

"Spencer Phyffe," Spencer said. "I came with the piano."

"Oh, yes. Glad you could make it," Mr. Carrington replied. "Remember, you can come for that piano anytime Monday."

Spencer smiled and nodded, and we moved on. Now that I had survived the receiving line, I looked around eagerly. The ballroom was brilliantly lit by half a dozen crystal chandeliers. On the dance floor, the girls' multicolored dresses contrasted with the dark tuxedos and dress uniforms of their partners. At the far end of the ballroom on a raised platform, an orchestra played the big-band dance tunes of an earlier era. I had been to high-school dances, but nothing in my past experience had prepared me for this.

"Not your basic Saturday night sock hop, that's for sure," Spencer remarked, echoing my thoughts aloud. "Want to dance?"

I glanced around nervously as he led the way onto the crowded dance floor, but there was no need for me to worry. There were so many people and so much activity in the room that no one paid any attention to us. And when Spencer wrapped his arm around my waist and drew me close, all my worries seemed to melt away. No matter what happened later, it was worth the risk. I would remember this night for the rest of my life.

For a while, everything was perfect. The contestants from Delaware, Colorado, and Arizona danced by with their partners but, like Mr. Carrington, they didn't recognize me. Then Jillian Reed, Virginia's contestant, waltzed by in the arms of a handsome cadet. Her eyes met mine for a moment, and she gave me a puzzled smile.

Clarissa's sash! I suddenly realized. I had been having such a wonderful time dancing with Spencer that I had forgotten all about it! As soon as the music ended, I excused myself, telling Spencer that I would return in time for the next dance. But before I could get away, two girls approached me.

"Wendy!" Vicky Johnson, of Kansas, said.

"I never expected to see you here! Boy, those pageant planners think of everything, don't they?"

I held my breath. If she asked me to pin her hem or fix her zipper, I would die on the spot. Then her companion, Michigan's Daphne Wilson, stared at the sash.

"Wendy, why are you wearing—"

"I was just going to the ladies' room," I cut in. "Why don't you both come with me?"

My brain was spinning. I would have to tell them something, but not here—not in front of Spencer. I had noticed rest rooms on the second floor, but since they were closer to the ballroom, they would probably be a lot busier than the ones downstairs. So I led the way out and down the stairs, searching frantically for any reason that would sound halfway convincing. Vicky was a sweet girl, but she loved to gossip, and I was pretty sure that whatever I told her would be public knowledge in no time. As for Daphne, I didn't know her as well, but I couldn't afford to trust anyone. When we reached the first floor ladies' room, I dashed into one of the stalls and locked the door.

"All right, Wendy," Daphne called from the other side of the door. "What's going on?"

"First you've got to promise not to tell," I warned, stalling for time. "It's top secret."

"We promise," both girls assured me.

I slipped off the incriminating sash and hung it from the hook on the back of the door. As I came out, I had a sudden inspiration. "Okay. I'm really not supposed to tell anybody this, but—but I'm not really a seamstress," I said. "I'm a reporter for a major national magazine, and I've gone undercover to get an inside look at the America's Teen Beauty Pageant."

"Wow!" Vicky said, obviously impressed.

"But you're so *young*," Daphne marveled. "How did you get that kind of a job at your age?"

"I'm not as young as I look," I said loftily, getting into the spirit of things. "I just finished my degree in journalism. They gave me this assignment because I look young enough to pass for a contestant."

"You sure do!" Vicky exclaimed. "I never would have guessed!"

"But what about Clarissa?" Daphne asked.

"How is she going to get into the ball now that you've taken her place?"

"She decided not to come, remember? Now, if you don't mind, I have to be getting back to the ballroom."

Taffeta skirts swishing, I sailed through the door into the foyer before they could ask any more questions. Just as I reached the foot of the stairs, the rest room door flew open and Vicky and Daphne came hurrying out. Vicky carried a long white strip of satin.

"Don't forget this, Wendy," she called after me. "You might need it."

"Thanks," I said without enthusiasm, taking the sash and slipping it over my head.

I went slowly up the stairs to the ballroom, wondering how long I could wait before trying to dispose of the sash again. The darned thing was harder to get rid of than the common cold! I was on my way to rejoin Spencer when Mrs. Forsythe, the former Florida girl, waylaid me. My heart sank.

"*There* you are!" she exclaimed. "I've been wanting to speak with you ever since I saw the list of contestants. I never dreamed that a relative of William Devoe would be representing Florida in the pageant this year. Why, Dr. Devoe was our family physician for years! Tell me, how is he?"

"Oh, he's fine," I assured her. No matter what sort of shape the man was in, he was probably better off than I was at the moment.

"Does his back still give him trouble?"

"To tell you the truth, I don't know, Mrs. Forsythe," I confessed. "I'm afraid we're rather distantly related."

"Really?" Mrs. Forsythe's eyebrows drew together in a puzzled frown. "But the newspaper said he was your *father*!"

Uh-oh! "Well, yes, but we—uh—we were never very close," I stammered.

For a moment, Mrs. Forsythe looked mystified. Then, to my astonishment, she began to laugh. "Oh my dear, you *are* your father's daughter! I was thinking you must take after your mother's side of the family—you don't look much like the Devoes. But you've certainly got your father's sense of humor! 'Never very close' indeed! What would your mother say?"

She was still laughing as she walked away, and I knew I had narrowly escaped disaster.

111

I found Spencer a moment later, drinking punch and watching the dancers.

"Finally!" he said as soon as he saw me. "I was beginning to wonder if I should send out a search party."

I smiled apologetically. "Sorry. It took a little longer than I expected."

"I've been sampling the refreshments while you were gone," Spencer said. "I even got you some punch."

As we sipped our drinks, I noticed several of the girls giving me curious looks, and one even pointed straight at me. I was frightened at first, until I heard someone whisper something about "undercover reporter" and "national magazine." Vicky had obviously told everyone about my "top secret" identity—just as I had hoped she would. The situation was getting more complicated by the minute, but at least I was no longer in danger of exposure. When Spencer and I returned to the dance floor, I felt more at ease than I had all evening.

But we had scarcely made more than a couple of turns on the floor when a commotion near the front of the room drew my eyes to the big double doors. What I saw made me freeze in Spencer's arms.

There, surrounded by three uniformed security guards, was Clarissa Devoe! I was too far away to hear what she was saying, but even at this distance it was obvious that Clarissa was throwing a tantrum. She pointed at one of the security guards, then at the white satin sash crossing the front of her pink satin gown. I didn't need sound effects to know that the guards weren't going to let her in. This event already had one contestant from Florida—me.

"What's the matter, Wendy?" he asked.

"N-nothing. I was just—uh—admiring Miss Georgia's gown."

By turning my head slightly, I discovered I could keep an eye on Clarissa's reflection in the mirrored walls. She was scanning the ballroom, obviously in search of the impostor, and I was thankful that Spencer's height concealed me, and the sash, from Clarissa's piercing gaze. Then Spencer twirled me around in time to the music, and at that moment Clarissa turned to the nearest guard and tugged at his arm, pointing an accusing finger in my direction. In the next instant, all three guards started purposefully across the ballroom with Clarissa at their heels.

"Spencer, I've got to go!" I cried.

"What's wrong!" he asked, a puzzled frown creasing his forehead.

"I can't explain! It's just that—*good-bye*!"

Spencer's grip on my hand tightened as I tried to back away. "But Wendy—"

I didn't wait to hear more. I pulled my hand out of his grasp, picked up my blue taffeta skirts, and fled.

# Ten

A green exit sign glowed on the side of the orchestra platform, and I headed in that direction, pushing and shoving my way past the dancing couples. The only thing that mattered now was getting away from the glamorous world to which I didn't belong, and from the boy who could never be mine.

At last I reached the exit. Throwing my weight against the door, I plunged through the opening into a long hallway. I threw a frantic glance down the length of the hall, first left, then right. There was a door at the end of the hall to my right, so I sprinted toward it.

Just outside the door was a steep, metal fire escape. Pausing only long enough to hitch my skirts up higher, I stumbled down the steps and into the night.

I had almost reached the corner of the building when someone grabbed my arm. I whirled around in terror, and discovered that my captor wasn't a security guard.

"Spencer! It's only you!" I sobbed, collapsing against his chest.

"I'm not sure, but I don't think that remark was particularly complimentary," Spencer said, wrapping his arms around me. "It's okay, Wendy. You've lost them."

Suddenly I came to my senses. This awful evening wasn't over yet, and I still had a part to play.

"Lost who?" I asked, slipping out of Spencer's embrace.

"Whoever it is you're running away from."

"How silly," I said with a feeble laugh. "What makes you think I'm running away from anyone?"

"Are you kidding? After the way you lit out

of that ballroom? You're either running from somebody, or your dress turns into rags at midnight."

Actually, he was closer to the truth than he knew, on both counts.

"It's nothing like that," I lied. "I just—had to get out of there."

"Yeah, so I noticed. Why?"

"Well, because it was hot and crowded and—and I had a headache."

"Do you always do wind sprints when you have a headache?" Spencer asked, raising his eyebrows. "Seems like it would be a lot easier to take a couple of aspirin."

"If you're trying to make me laugh, it won't work," I warned him, though I couldn't help smiling a little. "Okay, so I haven't got a headache. I admit it."

"Then what's wrong?" he asked, not teasing anymore.

I just shook my head.

"Wendy, if you're in some kind of trouble—" Spencer took my hands and drew me a step closer to him. "I'm not such a bad guy to talk to, you know," he said gently.

I looked up into his face, trying to read his

expression in the dim light. Even half-hidden by shadows, he looked so concerned that for a moment I was tempted to tell him everything. The only thing that held me back was the fear of seeing that look turn into one of—what? Contempt? Disgust? I couldn't bear it. I tore my eyes away from his and looked down.

"I—I think I just want to go home now," I murmured. "Would you mind picking up my bag?"

"Sure. I'll be right back."

Spencer returned a few minutes later and handed me my purse. As we walked in silence to his car, I took off the white satin sash and stuffed it into my evening bag.

My life as Florida's Teen Beauty was over.

When my alarm clock rang on Friday morning, all I wanted to do was turn it off and bury my head under the pillow. As long as I was asleep, I didn't have to think about the disastrous events of last night, or the prospect of facing Clarissa today. Still, I had a job to do, so I rolled out of bed and dressed for work.

I picked at my breakfast in silence, and Mom, noticing my glum mood, said, "Well, honey, you're awfully quiet today. Didn't you have a good time last night?"

"Oh, yes! It was great!" I said with false enthusiasm. "I'm just tired, that's all. Dancing for hours really takes it out of you."

"I'm glad you enjoyed yourself," Mom said, giving me a steady look. "By the way, I heard some interesting news on the radio this morning. It seems that someone tried to gate-crash the Teen Beauty Ball by posing as a contestant. Security guards tried to question her, but she escaped."

"Boy, some people really have a lot of nerve, don't they?" I croaked weakly.

"Wendy, I think you know more about this than you're letting on," Mom said. "That was you, wasn't it? You never really told Spencer at all."

My eyes filled with tears of shame. "I was going to, Mom, really I was," I said miserably. "But the time was never right, and then Spencer bought a ticket to the ball, and I just *couldn't* tell him after that! And Clarissa said she wasn't going, so I thought maybe— And it worked for a while but then everything went all wrong!" A big tear rolled down my cheek and splashed into my cereal bowl.

I felt miserable. The damage was done, and there was no way to undo it. How could I have guessed when I met Spencer on the stage that it would end like this?

I arrived at the Coliseum just as the girls were gathering for their last rehearsal. It would be a short session that would break at noon. I wasn't really surprised to see Clarissa break away from the group and hurry over to me.

"Wendy!" she called as she approached. "I want to talk to you!"

My stomach twisted itself into a hard knot. "Clarissa, I—"

Before I could finish my sentence, she cut me off. "Wendy, I'm so sorry about last night! Vicky told me all about it after you left, and I could just *die*! I never meant to blow your cover, but those guards were treating me like a *criminal* or something, and I just lost my head. Anyway, I hope I didn't cause you too much trouble."

"Don't—don't mention it," I stammered.

"It never occurred to me to mention that I'd changed my mind about coming to the ball," she continued. "My host mother's next-door neighbor owns a formal-wear shop here in Bellevue, and when she heard about my problem, she let me take my choice of any dress in stock! Anyway, I hope that you're not so upset with me that you won't mention me in your article." Clarissa gave me a big, warm smile. Then she whirled around and returned to her group.

Completely stunned by this unexpected turn of events, I wandered into the sewing room, where I found Mrs. Evans and Mrs. Crowley.

"Oh, Wendy," Mrs. Evans said, looking up from the dress she was pressing, "Mr. Carrington was just here. He wants to know how you want to be paid. He can leave your last paycheck here for you to pick up tomorrow, or you can get it Monday morning."

I started to say Monday would be fine, but then I remembered that Mr. Carrington had told Spencer last night that he could get the piano anytime Monday. I couldn't stand the thought of running into him. I was sure he had to have heard about the "gate-crasher" by now.

"I think I'd like to pick it up tomorrow, if that's all right," I said.

"Fine," said Mrs. Evans. "I'll tell Mr. Carrington."

By six o'clock that evening, everything was in an uproar. I was grateful to be kept so busy—it didn't leave me any time to think. When the contestant from Wisconsin lost one of her long white gloves, I found it inside her swimsuit, of all places. When Miss Connecticut's zipper broke just minutes before her beauty walk, I was the one who basted her formal gown back together. In between these major crises, there were the usual ripped hems, split seams, and loose sequins to be dealt with.

It was after eleven o'clock by the time the winners were announced. I was exhausted, but I couldn't help feeling proud when Connecticut's Teen Beauty was declared the winner. After all, it had been my emergency basting job that had prevented her gown from falling off! The contestant from South Dakota was named first runner-up, Jillian Reed of Virginia was second, and third runner-up was none other than Clarissa Devoe. Unless Spencer's TV was broken, there was no way he could have missed this.

After the pageant was over, Mrs. Evans, Mrs. Crowley, and I hung up the gowns the girls had discarded and draped them in plastic bags. By the time I got to my house, it was after midnight and I was exhausted. I dragged myself up the stairs and tumbled into bed, thankful that I was too worn-out to worry about where a certain boy was and what he was thinking.

# Eleven

On Saturday morning, I awoke heavy-eyed from a deep but not very restful sleep. Throwing on my oldest shorts and T-shirt, I dragged myself to the Coliseum, eager to pick up my last paycheck and put an end to this painful chapter of my life as soon as possible.

But once I got there and had the check in my hands, I hesitated, unwilling to walk out the door and leave this place where all the magic—and all the misery—had begun. Before I left, I had to see it all just one more time.

First I went to the stage area, where the pageant had taken place last night and where Spencer and I had met almost three weeks earlier. The piano still stood on the empty stage, draped in a large white sheet to protect it from damage. The effect was strange, almost ghostlike. The only people in sight were the electricians and stagehands, dismantling the special equipment they had installed for the pageant.

The backstage area was completely empty, and my footsteps echoed as I made my way down the hallway. It looked so different now, without the beautiful girls and their glamorous clothes.

I guess it was only natural that I eventually found myself in Clarissa's empty dressing room. I studied my reflection in the large mirror, taking in my oversize T-shirt, baggy boxer shorts, and straggly ponytail. There was hardly any resemblance between this girl and the radiant me who had attended the Teen Beauty Ball. As for Clarissa, all that remained of her was a clothes hanger, a couple of plastic bags, a discarded lipstick, and—

A glimpse of something red drew my eyes

126

to the small trash basket in the corner. It was a withered rose, surrounded by white baby's breath and wilting greenery. *My rose!* How *dare* she throw it away! I fell to my knees in front of the trash basket and dug out my bouquet piece by piece. Maybe if I took it home and put it in water—

"Well, look who's here," a familiar voice said. "Cinderella, back among the ashes."

"Spencer!" I cried, whirling around. There he stood in the doorway, looking as handsome as ever in jeans and a blue-and-white-striped shirt that made his eyes look even bluer. "What—what are you doing here?"

"I was about to ask you the same question," he said. "I thought you'd be halfway to Florida by now."

Why was he playing games with me? Was he just being mean?

I rose stiffly, clutching the mangled bouquet. "I—I'm not going to Florida," I said bluntly.

Spencer's eyebrows rose in mock surprise. "*Never?* What will your parents say?"

Why was he torturing me like this? Why didn't he just tell me what he thought of me and get it over with? My eyes filled with tears, but my chin rose, and I answered, "They won't say anything, because I don't live in Florida. You know by now that my name isn't Clarissa Devoe, and I'm not Florida's Teen Beauty. In fact, I'm not anybody's Teen Beauty. My name is Wendy Miller, and I'm— at least, I *was*—a pageant seamstress."

Spencer didn't say anything for a moment. He just gazed steadily at me. Then slowly he crossed the tiny room and took me by the shoulders. "Wendy Miller, do you really think I haven't known that all along?"

I could only stare at him, speechless. I had imagined this scene and Spencer's reaction a million times, but never once had I imagined it like this. "You—you *knew*?" I managed, finding my voice at last. "But how—"

"Well, maybe I didn't know *all* along," Spencer interrupted. "I didn't have any real reason to doubt you at first. Maybe it was that guy at Angelo's, who was so sure he knew you, that first made me wonder. Or maybe it was because there was too much of a resemblance between you and your 'host mother' to be just a coincidence. By the way, she's the reason I'm here. I went to your house first, and your mom told me where to find you."

"But but you sent flowers to Clarissa the very next Monday!" I said, still trying to take it all in.

Spencer gave me a mischievous grin. "Oh, that. That was kind of a test. When Sunday's paper came out describing a girl who sounded absolutely nothing like you, I knew something weird was going on. By the way, I hope you don't really want to be an actress," he added. "I have a feeling you'd make a lousy one. Anyway, I decided to try to solve the mystery, so I had flowers sent to Clarissa Devoe just to find out what would happen. When you thanked me for them, you really threw me for a loop. I was sure you wouldn't know anything about them!"

"I wouldn't have, if I hadn't been in the parking lot when the florist's van drove up. I was the one who brought the flowers to Clarissa."

"Well, that explains it. Then after they showed the real Clarissa on TV—the rest was almost too easy."

"I guess it would have been a lot simpler if I'd just told you to begin with, huh?" I mumbled, hanging my head.

"Sure. But then I wouldn't have had the chance to play detective."

I looked up at him then. "But if you knew, why didn't you tell me?"

"I figured when you got ready for me to know, *you'd* tell *me.*" Spencer's expression grew serious. "But you didn't. Why didn't you, Wendy? Why did you keep on pretending? I thought we had the beginning of something really special."

"I wanted to tell you, Spencer. Really I did," I said earnestly. "It was just that—"

"That what?"

"I didn't think you'd be much interested in the hired help," I blurted out.

Spencer stared at me as if I'd slapped him. "Do you mind telling me what gave you that impression?"

" 'Why don't they hire some menial to do that sort of thing?' " I quoted. "Remember when you said that?"

"Okay, that was dumb, I admit," Spencer confessed. "I was trying to get you to tell me the truth, and I guess I overdid it a little. I knew you were mad—you hardly said another word to me on the way back to the Coliseum."

"I wasn't mad," I said. "I was hurt, but I guess I shouldn't have been surprised, considering who you are."

"Who I am?" Spencer asked, looking totally confused.

"You're a Phyffe."

"So?"

"You're a Phyffe," I repeated. "You go to a fancy private school, your family is wealthy, you live at The Magnolias, you—"

"Hold it! Whatever gave you that idea?"

Now it was my turn to be confused. "*You* did!" I cried. "That first day when we met onstage, you said you came with the piano."

Spencer's look of confusion slowly turned to understanding, then amusement. He began to chuckle. "Is *that* what you think? Wendy, my name isn't Spencer Phyffe, P-H-Y-F-F-E—it's Spencer Fife, F-I-F-E. And I came with the piano because I've got a summer job with B & B Movers!"

I could hardly believe my ears. "But you said your Jag was in the shop!"

"I was joking! I thought you knew that!"

"And you bought a ticket to the ball!"

"No, I didn't. Mr. Carrington gave my boss a pair of tickets for moving the piano. My boss knew that I was interested in one of the contestants, so he gave them to me."

My head was spinning, but I picked up on one word immediately. "Did you say a *pair* of tickets?"

"That's right," he said. "You had as much right to be at that ball as anybody else. I gave *two* tickets to the guy at the door. I knew you planned to try passing yourself off as Miss Florida, but I couldn't believe you'd actually get away with it, so I hung on to the stubs just in case. I didn't want you to get in trouble—I love you too much." Then he blushed and mumbled, "Maybe you don't want to hear that, but it's true."

I didn't say anything right away. I couldn't—I was too thrilled and delighted by what I had just heard. Spencer shifted his weight uncomfortably from one foot to the other.

"Is it that important to you?" he asked in a worried voice. "That I'm not rich, I mean?"

I looked up at him with glowing eyes, remembering when I'd told Kim that I wished Spencer was a little more average. Miraculously, I had my wish. Wendy Miller and Spencer *Phyffe* might not have had much of a future together, but for Wendy Miller and Spencer *Fife*, the possibilities were endless.

"I guess I can forgive you for not being a millionaire, if you can forgive me for not being a beauty queen," I said.

"It's a deal," he said. Then he took me in his arms and sealed the bargain with a long, delicious kiss. "Oh, and one more thing," he added. "The Phyffes' son is named Steadman. I met him the day we moved the piano. You wouldn't like him. He's not your type at all."

And as we laughed and kissed a second time, I decided that being plain old Wendy Miller was just fine with me. I wouldn't trade places with any other girl in the world!

First love . . . first kiss!

A terrific series that focuses firmly on that most important moment in any girl's life – falling in love for the very first time ever.

Available from wherever Bantam paperbacks are sold!

1. Head Over Heels by Susan Blake
2. Love Song by Suzanne Weyn
3. Falling for You by Carla Bracale
4. The Perfect Couple by Helen Santori

# HART & SOUL

by Jahnna N. Malcolm

A dynamic new detective duo!

Beautiful, intelligent Amanda Hart, editor-in-chief of the school newspaper at Sutter Academy, has nothing in common with streetwise Mickey Soul, a gorgeous guy from the tough side of town. Yet, from the moment Mick swaggers into Mandy's life, she knows that nothing will ever be the same again! What brings them together is a mystery – but what keeps them together is purely a matter of heart and soul.

A contemporary, sophisticated series that is full of suspense.

1. KILL THE STORY
2. PLAY DEAD
3. SPEAK NO EVIL
4. GET THE PICTURE
5. TOO HOT TO HANDLE
6. SIGNED, SEALED, DELIVERED